S0-BZT-338

# Pig Kahuna

## Jennifer Sattler

SCHOLASTIC INC.
New York  Toronto  London  Auckland
Sydney  Mexico City  New Delhi  Hong Kong

No part of this publication may be reproduced, stored in a retrieval system, or transmitted in any
form or by any means, electronic, mechanical, photocopying, recording, or otherwise, without
written permission of the publisher. For information regarding permission, write to
Bloomsbury USA Children's Books, 175 Fifth Avenue, New York, NY 10010.

ISBN 978-0-545-44875-8

Copyright © 2011 by Jennifer Sattler. All rights reserved. Published by Scholastic Inc.,
557 Broadway, New York, NY 10012, by arrangement with Bloomsbury USA Children's Books.
SCHOLASTIC and associated logos are trademarks and/or registered trademarks of Scholastic Inc.

12 11 10 9 8 7 6 5 4 3 2          12 13 14 15 16 17/0

Printed in the U.S.A.                    08

This edition first printing, May 2012

Art created with acrylics and colored pencil
Typeset in Birdlegs
Book design by Nicole Gastonguay

For Paul

It was Saturday. Fergus and his baby brother, Dink, were collecting treasures.

The waves would roll in, leave something for their collection, and roll back out again. It worked quite nicely as long as Fergus didn't have to go in the water.

He knew there was more than
just treasure in that water.

There was a
lurking,
murky
ickiness.

So far that day Fergus and Dink
had collected:

some seaweed,

a pebble that looked
like an eyeball,

and a shell that *might*
be an actual shark's tooth.

They waited fifteen whole minutes, but nobody came to claim the surfboard. So they decided to make it the star of their collection.

Of course, surfing on it was out of the question because of the lurking, murky ickiness factor of the water.

So they found other, drier uses for it.

And they named it Dave.

Dave was a loyal companion. "Stay. Good boy."

After a while, Fergus offered to get some ice cream. "Chunky chocolate Chattanooga chew-chew chip, right, Dink?"

Dink looked long
and hard at Dave.

He seemed to have lost his shine.

"You miss the ocean, huh, big fella?
You should be wild! And free!"

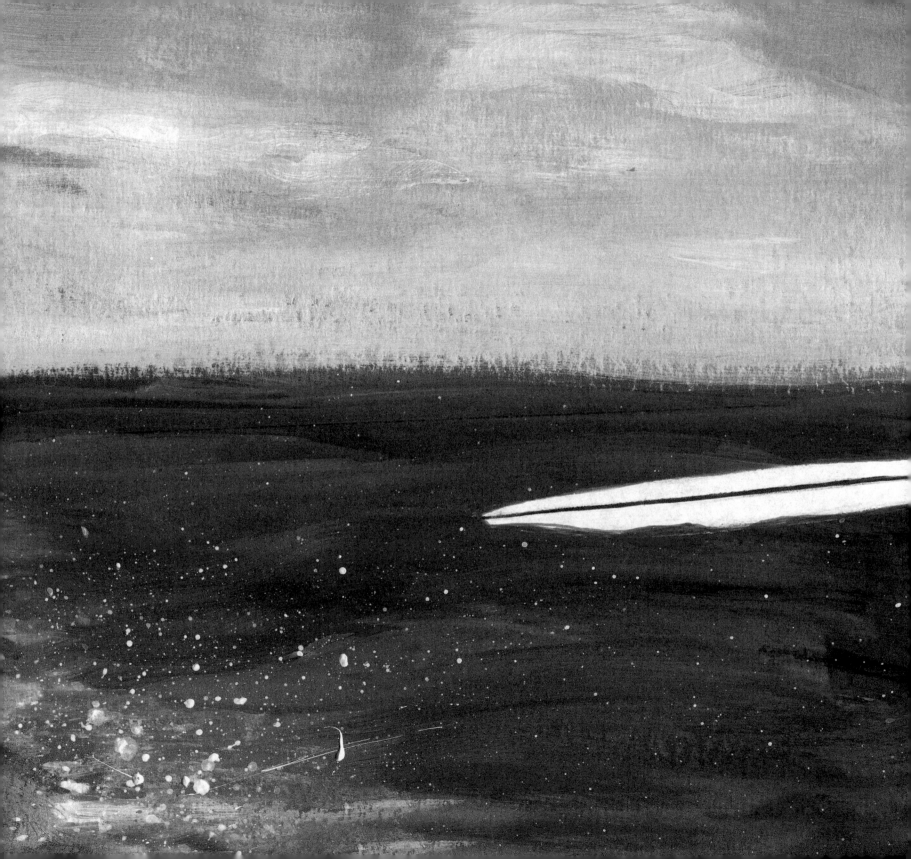

Fergus ran into the water and furiously swam out to save Dave.

Bon voyage!

"Don't worry, little buddy," he whispered.

No sooner had the words left
Fergus's mouth than he felt
Dave rise up beneath him.

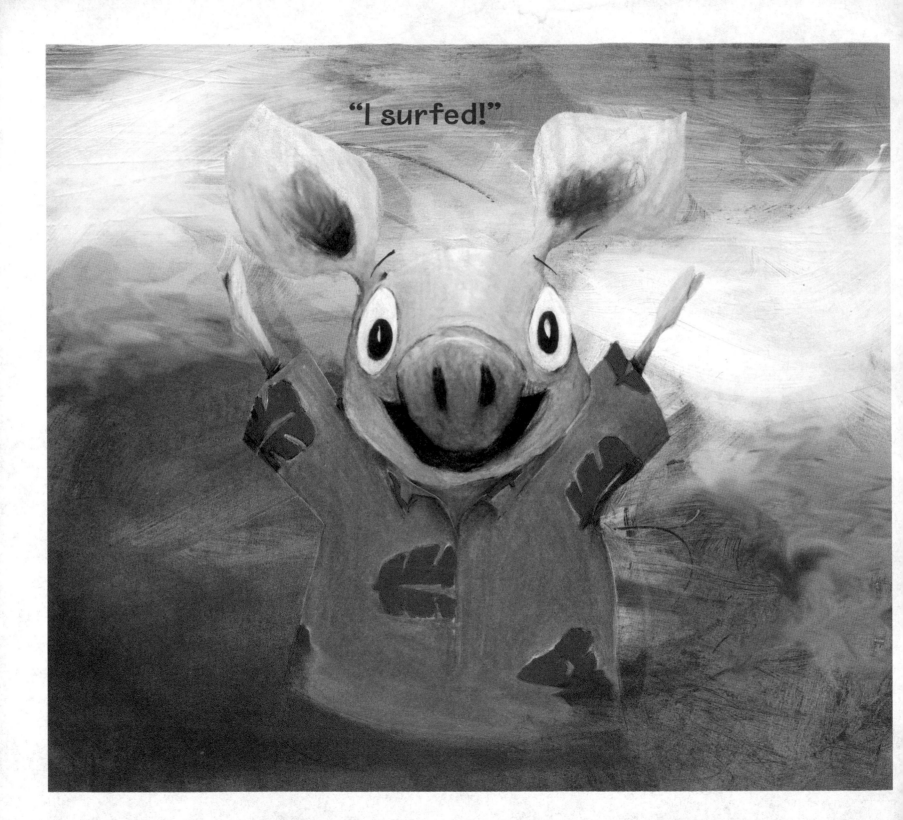

Fergus and Dink kept their eyes
peeled for more treasures.

And, boy, did they find one.